"Roll around in mud like you?"
said Heidi. "Pigs might fly!"

So far from all the other pigs,
Heidi hid away.
Lounging in the meadow flowers,
she passed one summer's day.

She stared into her mirror,
thinking she looked fine.
She polished up her toenails
till each one had a shine.

Then slowly in the twilight
she trundled off to bed.
And in the hay she gently laid
her sleepy little head.

Then Heidi fell asleep
and dreamed of nice hotels,

Of bubble baths and manicures
away from farmyard smells.

But at last the farmyard rooster crowed
his "Cock-a-doodle-doo.
It's time to rise, open your eyes,
the day is bright and new."

So Heidi took her morning stroll
above the mud-filled pen.
Grinning at the other pigs,
she walked along, but then—

The dog began his barking,
and he barked with all his might.
This caused the geese to panic,
and the ducks flew up in fright.

"Look out!" cried the other pigs
as some birds came flying by.
Then Heidi lost her balance
and fell into the sty!

The mud was awful gooey,
sort of sticky, blackish brown.
It covered her all over
and splashed her up and down.

And everyone admired her
in her chauffeur-driven car.
She appeared on all the talk shows,
just like a movie star.

"Heidi, you're the perfect pig,"
they said, "a model for the rest.
And if we had to rate you,
we'd say you are the best!"

No sign of nice pink piggy,
she was plastered from ear to ear.
From snuffling snout to curly tail,
she was covered front to rear.

And believe it or not, Heidi didn't cry,
she didn't whine or pout.
Instead she kicked her feet in mud
and gave this little shout:

"This lovely, slimy, gloopy stuff
is really very nice.
I never guessed that mud could be
a piggy's paradise!

"The way it feels between my toes
just makes me want to sing.
It makes me want to roll around
and wallow till evening."

So Heidi stayed and wallowed,
rolling in the mire.
And mud became a special thing;
it was her heart's desire.

Now Heidi's like the other pigs;
she can't stand being clean.
But when it comes to filthiness,
happy Heidi is the queen!